A HAN & CHEWIE ADVENTURE

WRITTEN BY
CAVAN SCOTT

ILLUSTRATED BY
ELSA CHARRETIER

Disney

LUCASFILM
P R E S S

LOS ANGELES • NEW YORK

CALGARY PUBLIC LIBRARY

AUG   2019

© & TM 2018 Lucasfilm Ltd.

All rights reserved. Published by Disney • Lucasfilm Press,
an imprint of Disney Book Group. No part of this book may be reproduced or transmitted in
any form or by any means, electronic or mechanical, including photocopying, recording, or by
any information storage and retrieval system, without written permission from the publisher.

For information address Disney • Lucasfilm Press,
1200 Grand Central Avenue, Glendale, California 91201.

Printed in the United States of America

First Paperback Edition, April 2018

1 3 5 7 9 10 8 6 4 2

FAC-029261-18072

ISBN 978-1-368-01624-7

Library of Congress Control Number on file

Designed by Leigh Zieske

SUSTAINABLE
FORESTRY
INITIATIVE

Certified Sourcing

www.sfiprogram.org
SFI-01415

If you purchased this book without a cover, you should be aware that this book is stolen
property. It was reported as "unsold and destroyed" to the publisher, and neither the
author nor the publisher has received any payment for this "stripped" book.

Visit the official *Star Wars* website at: www.starwars.com.

» ATTENTION, READER

Han Solo and his Wookiee copilot,
Chewbacca, are two of the galaxy's greatest
smugglers—but they need your help!

This book is full of choices—choices that
lead to different adventures, choices that you
must make to help Han and Chewie.

Do not read the following pages straight through
from start to finish! When you are asked to make
a choice, follow the instructions to see where
that choice will lead Han and Chewie next.

CHOOSE CAREFULLY.

AND MAY THE FORCE BE WITH YOU!

A LONG TIME AGO
IN A GALAXY FAR, FAR AWAY. . . .

"I'M TELLING YOU, CHEWIE," Han Solo said as he checked the flight controls. "This is easy money. The easiest we've ever made."

The *Millennium Falcon*'s cockpit was immediately filled with a barrage of disbelieving growls and grunts.

Han frowned at the Wookiee in the copilot's seat. "I mean it! All we have to do is deliver the cargo to Jabba. What's the problem?"

"HRRUUNGH," Chewbacca answered in his native language. Luckily, Han understood Shyriiwook. The problem was that Jabba the Hutt was one of the most dangerous crime lords in the galaxy. The last smuggler to cross the gruesome gangster had met an untimely end. Han still shuddered at the memory of the sound of crunching bones echoing around Jabba's throne room.

Taking a job from Jabba was always risky. Things had a habit of going wrong, but this time would be different. The *Millennium Falcon*'s cargo hold was packed with crates of stolen Imperial tech. Han didn't know why Jabba wanted the tech, and he cared even less. He just wanted to get paid.

Han checked the navicomputer and prepared to make a course correction.

"Trust me, will you?" he told Chewie. "I've got a good feeling about this."

With the flick of a lever, the *Falcon* dropped out of hyperspace. A sea of sparkling stars stretched out in front of them.

It would have been beautiful if not for the flotilla of imposing starships that blocked their path.

"It's an Imperial blockade!" Han shouted as he

slammed on the reverse engines, bringing the *Falcon* to an emergency stop.

"What's the Empire doing here?"

Three Imperial *Gozanti*-class cruisers formed a checkpoint between the *Falcon* and the planets beyond, along with a Star Destroyer, two frigates, and countless TIE fighters that darted among the larger ships like angry wasps.

A light flashed on the comm. A message was coming through.

"*Unidentified cruiser, this is Blockade Control,*" crackled a clipped voice. "*You are not transmitting your ID code.*"

There was a reason for that. All ships were required to automatically broadcast an IFF code, which identified them as a friend or a foe.

Han had deactivated the *Falcon's* transmitter long before, after winning the ship from fellow smuggler Lando Calrissian in a game of sabacc.

Han liked to keep a low profile.

He clicked a button to reply.

"Er, that's an affirmative, Control. We have a fault in our transponder. Been meaning to get it fixed."

"*Transmit your IFF now.*"

Han could almost feel the Imperial cannons locking on to his position.

"Sure," he agreed, trying to sound cheerful. "Stand by for transmission."

Muting the comm, he turned to Chewie. "Do we have any IFF codes?"

Chewie responded with a growl.

"You bought codes from *Azmorigan*? Are you *crazy*? The guy's a crook."

"*HRRAARH!*"

"Yeah, I know *we're* crooks, but at least we're *honest* crooks."

4

The same couldn't be said of Azmorigan. Han had been double-crossed by the Jablogian more times than he cared to remember, but he was running out of time.

There was no guarantee Azmorigan's codes would even work, but it was either that or blast their way through the blockade.

WHAT SHOULD HAN DO?

IF YOU THINK HE SHOULD USE AZMORIGAN'S CODES, TURN TO PAGE 10.
IF YOU THINK HE SHOULD BLAST HIS WAY THROUGH THE IMPERIAL BLOCKADE, TURN TO PAGE 13.

HAN OPENED FIRE, the *Falcon*'s quad cannons raking the cruiser's bow.

The Imperial ship shot back, but Han dropped into a roll, narrowly avoiding the volley of emerald green plasma. He streaked past the cruiser, heading for a gap between the two frigates. It was going to be tight. Possibly too tight.

Chewie understood what Han was planning to do and looked over at his friend in disbelief.

"Trust me," Han replied. "I've done this before. Kind of."

Realizing his foolhardy plan, the frigates started to move closer together, the gap narrowing by the second.

Han turned the ship on its side. The *Falcon* shot through the gap, so close that its sensor disk scraped the starboard frigate's hull.

But then they were through, soaring into clear space. Chewie roared in approval. They'd made it!

Or so they thought. In the excitement, they'd forgotten about the Star Destroyer. The colossal warship fired, its turbolasers finding their target.

The deadly energy struck the *Falcon* at point-blank

range, surging through its shields. Systems blew from bow to stern, and fires ignited all across the ship as power lines ruptured and circuits overloaded.

Han cried out as the console above his head exploded, a heavy panel dropping to pin him against the dashboard. Taking control of the ship, Chewbacca steered the *Falcon* away from the TIE fighters that had dropped into pursuit.

"WHRAA?"

"I'm fine," Han lied, shoving the twisted panel off his wounded shoulder. The ship shuddered as the nearest starfighter unloaded its lasers into their already damaged hull. Han imagined the TIE's black-clad pilot hunched over his targeting computer. He'd be searching for the quickest way to blast the *Falcon* into space dust.

Well, not today, pal, Han promised through his pain. The *Falcon* was about to fight back!

WHO SHOULD FIRE THE *FALCON'S* CANNONS—HAN OR CHEWBACCA?

IF YOU THINK IT SHOULD BE HAN, TURN TO PAGE 50. IF YOU THINK IT SHOULD BE CHEWIE, TURN TO PAGE 40.

CHEWIE GAVE HAN a shove toward the trees.

"All right. I'll go look, you big bloggin." Han drew his blaster. "Wait till Maz hears about this."

Something glinted up ahead. A speeder bike sat in a small clearing. Han recognized the model—a Caelii-Merced Skyblade-330. He hadn't seen one in years, not since his run-in with Enfys Nest's marauders. Keeping his eyes on the trees, he snuck forward, reaching for the engine. It was still warm.

Laser fire whistled past Han's ear. He ducked and rolled, taking cover behind a thick tree.

Han looked around the trunk to see who was firing. It was a young Twi'lek woman, dressed in leather and holding a snub-nosed blaster rifle. Not just any rifle—a Czerka 4000. Han knew the weapon. The power pack would need to recharge every nine shots. Cocking his own blaster, Han counted out her blasts, and on the ninth, he turned and fired at the woman's rifle.

DOES HAN MAKE THE SHOT?

NO—GO TO PAGE 38.

YES—GO TO PAGE 26.

HAN REOPENED THE CHANNEL. The controller wasn't happy.

"Unidentified ship. You will respond to this message. Repeat: you will respond, or we shall open fire."

"Okay, okay," Han replied. "Transmitting codes now."

Han checked the IFF codes in the computer. There were two to choose from. One would identify the *Falcon* as a medical transport, ferrying essential supplies to the Western Reaches. The other was for a consular ship on official business for the Imperial Senate. Neither was particularly believable. . . .

WHAT CODE SHOULD HAN CHOOSE?

THE MEDICAL SHIP—TURN TO PAGE 52.
THE DIPLOMATIC CRUISER—TURN TO PAGE 49.

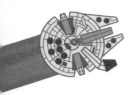

"HEY! WATCH IT!"

While Chewbacca was an excellent copilot, the Wookiee made for a lousy nurse. But he tried his best to apply bacta-soaked bandages to Han's shoulder.

"You sure you know what you're doing?"

Chewie pulled the bandages even tighter.

"Ow!" Han swatted Chewie's hand away. "Tell you what, I'll do it myself."

The bandages in place, Han pulled on his shirt. The *Falcon's* hull creaked ominously. Han put his hand on the nearest wall, feeling the vibrations through his palm. The old girl had taken a pummeling. Most of her systems were off-line, but at least they were safe, the autopilot guiding them through hyperspace.

Or so they thought.

The deck lurched violently beneath Han's feet, throwing him against Chewie.

"The hyperdrive's cut out," Han said as they raced for the cockpit, bouncing off the bulkheads with every shake and shudder. "I thought you fixed that thing."

He tumbled through the hatch, stopping short when he saw the huge flame-colored planet in front of them.

"We're caught in its gravitational pull," Han said, dropping into the seat in front of the flight controls. "Reverse engines. Full power."

They continued thundering toward the planet.

"I said full power!"

But it was no good. Han checked a readout.

"Propulsion systems have failed. There's no way to break free."

They were deep in the planet's atmosphere, plunging through clouds the color of molten lava.

If they couldn't escape the planet's atmosphere, they'd have to land. Most of the planet's surface seemed to be covered in dense jungle, the odd outcrop of jagged mountains rising from the trees.

Han was the best pilot he knew, but even he couldn't land a ship he could barely steer.

The only other option was to abandon ship. There was a chance that the escape pods wouldn't launch, but they had ejection packs stowed in the main hold.

Could he bear to abandon the *Falcon*?

WHAT DOES HAN DECIDE TO DO?

ABANDON SHIP—TURN TO PAGE 62.

TRY TO LAND—TURN TO PAGE 46.

12

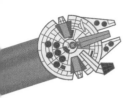

HAN KILLED THE COMM. "There's only one way we're getting past this blockade."

Before Chewbacca could stop him, Han gunned the engines and flew toward a gap in the ships. The maneuver was met by a barrage of Imperial energy bolts.

"*WHRAAA!*" bawled Chewbacca.

"Don't worry, the shields will hold," Han said, almost believing it. Ahead, a cruiser swung into a defensive position, the Star Destroyer looming directly behind. Han knew he'd have to attack one of them . . . but which one?

WHICH SHIP SHOULD HAN ATTACK?

THE STAR DESTROYER—TURN TO PAGE 36.

THE IMPERIAL CRUISER—TURN TO PAGE 6.

CHEWIE GLANCED NERVOUSLY at the trees.

Han gave the Wookiee a well-meaning slap on the arm. "Stop worrying. Whatever it is, it's probably more scared of us than we are of it."

They worked long into the night, securing the ship's exterior before getting ready to head inside.

Han threw down his goggles and stretched out his back. The bacta bandages had done their work, but he ached from head to foot. The rest of the repairs would have to wait for morning. Yawning, Han turned and found himself surrounded by a mob of armed strangers. There were eight of them total, each pointing a hefty blaster in his direction.

Maybe it hadn't been an ash-rabbit after all. . . .

DO HAN AND CHEWIE ESCAPE INTO THE
FALCON OR STAY AND FIGHT?

ESCAPE INTO THE _FALCON_—TURN TO PAGE 45.
STAY AND FIGHT—TURN TO PAGE 32.

"HRAAAH," ANSWERED CHEWIE.

"Was thinking the same thing myself," said Han, wrestling with the controls. Centimeter by painful centimeter, the *Falcon* banked toward the jungle.

Exotic birds burst from the thick canopy ahead of them, spooked by the *Falcon's* noisy descent. Han was pretty spooked himself. If he could just use the trees to cushion their landing . . .

"Here we go!"

The ship plowed into the trees. Trunks splintered like twigs, the ragged stumps tearing chunks of armor plating from the *Falcon's* bow.

Han and Chewie hung on to their controls as the cruiser carved a chaotic path through the jungle. Branches slammed against the viewport, and the ship finally made contact with the ground. The *Falcon* bounced once before skidding on its belly, gouging a deep trench.

With one final bone-shattering jolt, the ship shuddered to a halt, smoke billowing from its engines.

Han opened one eye cautiously. As far as he could tell, they were down and safe. Sunlight streamed

through the windows, the transparisteel miraculously free of cracks. He let out a whoop of joy and relief.

Forgetting Han's injuries, Chewbacca slapped him on the shoulder, but Han didn't care. They'd made it. That was all that mattered.

Now they just had to check the damage.

GO TO PAGE 21.

WARNING LIGHTS FLASHED all over the cockpit. That last strike had been bad. The *Falcon's* shields were failing, and at least a dozen power lines had blown.

"Chewie?" Han yelled into the comm. "Talk to me, pal."

A wail behind him nearly made Han jump out of his seat.

Han twisted around, ignoring the stabbing pain in his shoulder, as Chewie rushed back into the cockpit.

"WHHRAA!"

"I know the guns aren't working," Han replied, relieved his friend was okay, but snapping back to business. The remaining two starfighters had dropped into an attack run, ready to finish them off. "The power converters are smashed, and the shield generators are hanging on by a thread." The sudden blare of an alarm forced him to correct his diagnosis. "Okay, the shield generators are *gone*. This is gonna be bumpy."

Han threw the ship into a spin as the TIE fighters came out of nowhere, their lasers missing the *Falcon* by a hair. Han grimaced as he tried to pull around. His shoulder felt like it was on fire and the controls were getting more sluggish by the second. Even with its armor plating, another direct hit would disable the *Falcon* once and for all.

"I'm gonna attempt lightspeed," Han said. It was their only chance. TIE fighters couldn't make the jump to hyperspace, and even if the rest of the blockade followed, the *Falcon* could outrun the fastest Imperial ship.

Priming the hyperdrive, Han gritted his teeth and yanked back the control. There was a jolt and a shudder, and the hyperdrive panel exploded beneath Han's hand.

"Well, that's just perfect," Han said, blowing on his scorched fingers. "Now the hyperdrive's gone, too."

Chewie counted the number of TIE fighters that were now on their tail. Han stopped him when he got to seven.

"How's about you do something more useful, huh? Like getting the weapons back up and running again."

But Chewie had another idea. *"HHRAAAGH."*

Han shook his head. "Repairing the hyperdrive will take too long. You'll have to reroute the field stabilizers and—"

"WRAAAH!"

"I hear you, buddy, but you don't have time to fix both. Weapons or hyperdrive. It's one or the other. . . ."

WHICH SYSTEM SHOULD CHEWIE FIX?

WEAPONS—TURN TO PAGE 47.

HYPERDRIVE—TURN TO PAGE 30.

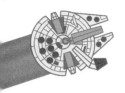

"WELL, I'VE SEEN WORSE. . . ."

They were standing in the clearing the *Falcon* had carved through the trees. While Chewie sifted through the debris, Han walked a wide circle around his ship.

The starfighters' lasers had blackened the *Falcon*'s hull, but a few scorch marks didn't bother Han. The main repairs were going to take time, and they were missing a few essential components. The crash had damaged the power core's primary heat exchanger. Han was convinced the ship could still get them off-planet, but Chewie wasn't so sure.

They went to work, starting with the hull. Chewie crouched beneath the ship, welding cracks in the armor plating, while Han climbed up top to repair the fuel line to the primary cannon.

They worked in silence, the stillness of the jungle punctuated by the calls of strange birds and the monotonous chirp of insects. It was peaceful, almost calming. It was a pleasant change from being shot at.

CRACK!

Han looked up at the sound of splintering wood.

He peered into the trees for a moment before clambering down to Chewbacca.

"You hear that?"

Chewie nodded, wiping his hands on an oily rag.

Han's hand dropped instinctively to the blaster he wore in a holster on his right leg. "What do you think it was? A wild animal?"

CRACK!

There it was again, behind them that time. Han spun around.

"*WHRAAAH,*" Chewie grumbled.

Han's eyebrows shot up. "You want *me* to go? You're the one who can rip arms out of their sockets! Besides, for all we know it's just an ash-rabbit or something. Imagine that—the big bad Wookiee scared of a little bunny."

Han was uneasy, too, although he would never admit it. They were being watched; he was sure of it.

SHOULD HAN INVESTIGATE?

**NAH, IT'S PROBABLY JUST AN
ASH-RABBIT—TURN TO PAGE 14.
YEAH, YOU CAN NEVER BE TOO
CAREFUL—TURN TO PAGE 8.**

IT WAS AN UTTERLY terrible idea.

The *Falcon*'s cargo belonged to Jabba the Hutt. Jabba would react badly if any of it didn't reach Tatooine. In fact, the overgrown space slug would probably rip Han's head from his shoulders.

But hey, what use was a head if Han was atomized by a squad of TIE fighters first?

"Jabba will understand," he told himself as he punched a series of buttons above his head. "He's an understanding guy. Right?"

The computer beeped that it was ready.

Han put a finger on his comlink. "Chewie? You better hang on to something. I'm about to do something stupid."

"*RAAAH?*" Chewie asked over the comm.

"*Really* stupid," Han confirmed, and jabbed one final control.

Behind the *Falcon*, the TIE fighters dropped into a standard attack formation. They were almost in range, the squadron leader eager to take the shot himself.

He smiled behind his black helmet, the expression faltering as their prey's airlock suddenly opened.

Crates streamed from the back of the *Millennium Falcon*.

Large crates.

Heavy crates.

Solid crates.

Before he could pull up, the leader's TIE fighter barreled into the dumped cargo and exploded on impact.

Han didn't watch his improvised minefield reduce the rest of the TIE fighters to scrap. He was too busy trying to close the airlock.

The *Falcon* was decompressing; the air inside the ship was getting sucked through the open door into the cold vacuum of space. At that rate, everything in the *Falcon* would get dragged with it—Han included!

With a final cry of defiance, Han slapped his hand down on the override.

The airlock sealed, and all was calm.

Han panted heavily as an indicator over his head flashed from red to blue.

The hyperdrive was working again.

"Good work, Chewie!" Han cheered, rerouting the hyperdrive controls to another panel in front of him.

Chewie responded by asking what had happened to the cargo.

"Jabba won't mind," Han replied. "What's a few crates among friends?"

The *Millennium Falcon* leapt into hyperspace. They had run the Imperial blockade and survived.

TURN TO PAGE 11.

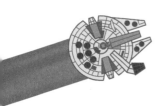

HAN'S SHOT STRUCK the rifle, jolting it out of the woman's hands, but she darted into the jungle before Han could stun her with another blaster shot. Then he heard a familiar roar.

Han found the woman struggling to escape from Chewbacca, who had her in an easy headlock.

"Nice shot," she snarled as Han swaggered toward her.

He didn't have time for chitchat.

"Who are you?"

"I could ask the same question," the woman retorted.

When he didn't reply, she reluctantly answered: "Meecha Odon, Meech to my friends."

"Friends don't spy on each other."

She smirked. "Didn't say we were friends . . . yet."

Han grinned back, letting his gun drop. Meech took the opportunity to kick at him. He stepped back, avoiding her booted foot.

"Nice try, kid. I like you. You and me *could* be pals . . ."

"If I told you where I came from?" the woman guessed.

He spread his hands. "See? We're getting along great."

Meech nodded past Han's shoulder.

"Nodo's shipyard, a couple kilometers or so that way."

He exchanged knowing looks with Chewie.

"A shipyard, eh?"

"Nodo can fix anything." She glanced back at the *Falcon*. "Even that heap of junk."

He ignored the jab. "Seems a strange place to open a business. Can't get much passing trade."

She shrugged. "People know where he is."

"The *right* people."

Meech sighed. "Not usually."

Han understood. "A chop shop. Makes sense. Visited a few in my time." It wasn't a lie. Chop shops handled stolen ships, stripping them down for parts. Most of the *Falcon*'s systems had come from such dives, far from prying Imperial eyes.

Chewbacca let out a series of grunts.

Meech looked up at the Wookiee. "What did he say?"

"Relax. He's not going to hurt you. Not unless you make another crack about our ship."

"But you need something?"

She was a smart one.

"A heat exchanger," Han replied.

Meech seized on the new information. "Nodo will have one, definitely."

"And you can persuade him to part with it?"

Then she didn't look so sure. "For the right price."

Han holstered his blaster. "We're running low on credits." He looked in the direction of the abandoned speeder bike. "But if this Nodo guy has one to spare . . ."

Meech's eyes went wide as she realized what Han was suggesting. "You're going to steal one? From *Nodo*?"

"Not steal," Han insisted. "Borrow. On a long-term loan. He won't even notice it's gone."

"I could help."

He laughed at the suggestion. "And raise the alarm as soon as my back's turned? I don't think so. Besides, I work better on my own."

Chewbacca wailed mournfully.

Han rolled his eyes. "You know what I mean." He jabbed a finger at Meech. "Deal with her?"

She paled. "Deal with me *how*?"

"No need to panic. Chewie's just going to make sure you can't warn your pals. Don't worry, we'll let you go before we blast off." He gave the woman a lopsided grin. "Mind if I use your speeder?"

Meech struggled. "Do I have a choice?"

Han called over his shoulder as he disappeared through the trees: "What are friends for?"

GO TO PAGE 54.

HAN WAS RUNNING OUT of options. In cases like this, he had to do what he always did best . . . lie!

"You want the name? Why didn't you say so? The planet's called, um . . . um . . ."

Why couldn't he think of any names? He looked at Chewie, but the Wookiee was no help.

Han said the first thing that came into his head.

"Fuzzballia!" he spluttered. "Fuzzballia Seven."

The other end of the comm was silent. For a moment, Han thought his bluff was going to work, that the blockade controller would be so bored with the conversation she would wave the *Falcon* through.

But then a tractor beam burst from the nearest Star Destroyer, locking them in place. Han tried to break the *Falcon* free, but the beam was too strong. He had gambled and lost.

Jabba would never get his cargo now.

THE END

CAN YOU GO BACK AND HELP HAN
MAKE A BETTER DECISION?
WHERE WILL THE ADVENTURE LEAD NEXT TIME?

HAN RAISED HIS HANDS in surrender as Chewie continued to argue. "Okay, you win. Fix the hyperdrive. Anything to shut you up."

Chewbacca grabbed his tools and bustled out of the cockpit.

"There's no need to worry," Han told himself. "Chewie can fix anything. I taught him everything he knows."

He glanced at the rear monitors. The TIEs were gaining fast. He needed to buy Chewie more time, but how?

He did have one idea, but he was pretty sure it would never work. . . .

WHAT DOES HAN DO?

**DUMP THEIR CARGO IN SPACE TO CREATE
A DISTRACTION—TURN TO PAGE 23.**
**POWER DOWN THE ENGINES AND PRETEND
TO SURRENDER—TURN TO PAGE 44.**

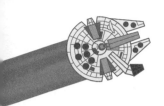

THEIR BLASTERS MAY HAVE been bigger, but Han was a quicker draw. The mob scattered as he fired, stunning a large Hylobon in their number. The alien went down, his rifle skittering across the ground. Chewie snatched it up and returned fire, taking out two more of their assailants.

Maybe luck was on their side.

Maybe not.

It soon became clear that the mob wasn't alone. More and more aliens came streaming out of the trees. Tall, short, thick, and thin . . . and all wielding powerful weapons. Han and Chewbacca were outnumbered and outgunned.

Han yelled for Chewie to get on board, but it was too late. A stun bolt streaked from the trees, hitting Han squarely in the chest.

His legs crumpled beneath him and he collapsed. He moaned as rough hands dragged him in front of the group's leader.

The alien belonged to a species Han had never seen before, with four muscular arms and a crocodilian face smothered in green scales. He was wearing oily overalls complete with a patch proclaiming what Han could only assume was his name. Han tried to focus on the writing. His vision was still blurred, but he could just make out the letters: NODO.

"Who are you?" Nodo demanded, jabbing a thick finger at Han's chest. "And who d'ya work for?"

WHO DOES HAN SAY HE WORKS FOR?

HIMSELF—TURN TO PAGE 48.
JABBA THE HUTT—TURN TO PAGE 60.

IT SEEMED AS IF there was only one choice. The trees were too far away. They were going to have to take the *Falcon* down in the mountains.

Using the last of his strength, Han nudged the ship toward a rocky plateau. They were going in too fast, but there was little he could do about that. All he could do was point the *Falcon* in the direction of the jagged crags and hope for the best.

In his head, Han counted down the seconds to impact.

Five . . . four . . . three . . . two . . . one . . .

THOOM!

The ship slammed into the mountain, skidding hopelessly out of control. Han thought they were going to shoot over the other side and plunge to their doom, but the *Falcon* came to rest with a final mighty crunch. Han was thrown against the viewport and bounced back onto the deck. His ears were ringing, and colored spots danced across his vision, but he was alive . . . and so was Chewie.

Roaring with relief, the Wookiee pulled Han into

a bone-crunching hug, but Han didn't care, injured shoulder or not.

They were battered and bruised, but they'd survived.

That was more than could be said for the *Falcon*.

The mountainside was littered with debris. The ship's underside had been all but ripped away in the crash. There was no way they'd get it off the ground, not without help.

Reluctantly, Han fired up the emergency beacon and sent a distress call to Tatooine.

Hopefully, Jabba would send a rescue mission—not for them of course, but for his cargo.

The same cargo Han had dumped in space.

This was going to take a *lot* of explaining. . . .

THE END

CAN YOU GO BACK AND HELP HAN
MAKE A BETTER DECISION?
WHERE WILL THE ADVENTURE LEAD NEXT TIME?

HAN KNEW HE DIDN'T have time to waste.

Star Destroyers were huge and therefore moved slowly. He could blast the wedge-shaped battleship and be away before the behemoth even fired its maneuvering thrusters.

He banked toward the Star Destroyer, targeting the nearest defense turret.

The *Falcon* fired, scoring a direct hit. The gun turret detonated in a blaze of light.

But the Star Destroyer was still dangerous. Turbolasers strafed the *Falcon*'s hull.

Chewbacca roared as explosions racked the ship, the cockpit filling with thick choking smoke.

"Come on, baby!" Han cried, but the *Falcon*'s controls were dead. The Star Destroyer's attack had knocked out both the engines and defensive systems.

They were helpless.

Chewie bleated a warning, but Han already knew what was happening. The *Millennium Falcon* was being dragged into the Star Destroyer by a tractor beam. Soon they would be boarded by stormtroopers and arrested.

It was over . . . for now.

Han would find a way out of this.

He always did.

THE END

CAN YOU GO BACK AND HELP HAN

MAKE A BETTER DECISION?

WHERE WILL THE ADVENTURE LEAD NEXT TIME?

HAN'S SHOT WENT WIDE, missing the woman's rifle.

But the energy bolt cut deep into the tree behind her, slicing into the trunk like an axe. She turned just as it toppled forward, knocking her to the side.

"HRRRAUGH?" Chewbacca bellowed as he crashed into the clearing to find Han checking on the woman, who had been knocked unconscious by the falling tree.

"Now he arrives," Han said, grabbing a handful of vines. With a grunt, he ripped them free and threw them at the Wookiee. "Tie up her hands, will you?"

Chewie caught the vines and rumbled a question.

"How am I supposed to know where she came from?" Han replied. "What does it matter? We'll be long gone by the time she wakes up."

The repairs took longer than either of them expected. Night had fallen by the time Han scrambled out from beneath the *Falcon*'s undercarriage.

Yawning, he turned and found himself staring down the barrel of a blaster. His hand went to his holster, but before he could shoot, a laser bolt hit him in the chest. He was thrown back, stunned.

Hands grabbed him, dragging him in front of a pair of oversize black boots. He looked up to see a blurry figure above him. He could just make out two sets of muscular arms and a broad face covered in thick green scales. The reptilian was wearing dirty overalls complete with a patch proclaiming what Han could only assume was its name. Han tried to focus on the writing. His vision was still blurred, but he could just make out the letters: NODO.

"Who are you?" hissed the alien, glowering down at him. "And who do you work for?"

WHO DOES HAN SAY HE WORKS FOR?

HIMSELF—TURN TO PAGE 48.

JABBA THE HUTT—TURN TO PAGE 60.

"I'LL TAKE THE CANNONS," Han said, levering himself out of his seat. He didn't get far. Pain coursed through his shoulder, forcing him to shout out.

"WHHRRAGH!" Chewie bellowed as Han flopped helplessly back into the chair.

"You're right," Han admitted, clutching his throbbing arm. "I'll never be able to aim. You go."

The Wookiee charged out of the cockpit, heading for the *Falcon's* lower gun turret.

Reaching the rotating pod, Chewie grabbed the headset that would connect him to Han in the cockpit.

"Three of them, coming in fast," Han said over the comm. *"Teach those bucketheads a lesson."*

Activating the targeting system, Chewie grabbed hold of the firing grips. Another direct hit shook the ship, and a TIE fighter howled past Chewbacca's gun. Locking on to the starfighter, Chewie tracked its path and squeezed the triggers. The *Falcon's* cannons bucked, sending scarlet bolts screaming after the TIE. Chewbacca bellowed in frustration as the starfighter veered sharply to the left, the shots dissolving harmlessly in the void.

"You nearly had him, pal," Han yelled in his ear. *"Keep going."*

Chewbacca swiveled around, the targeting computer beeping as it once again zeroed in on the fighter. Chewie fired again, and this time the TIE erupted in a dazzling explosion.

"One down, two to go."

The last thing Chewie needed was a countdown from Han. He'd already spotted the second starfighter zooming in for the kill, and he had the Imperial pilot right where he wanted. There was no way Chewbacca could miss. With a satisfied grunt, Chewie squeezed the trigger.

Nothing happened.

There were no lasers. No explosions. Nothing.

Chewie tried again, shaking the firing grip, but the guns were dead.

The TIE fighter's lasers flared in the darkness.

TURN TO PAGE 18.

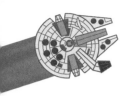

HAN CONSIDERED MAKING UP the name of a planet, but what was the point? If the officer knew the Western Reaches as well as she claimed, she'd see through the lie easily. Shutting down the comm, he cut off the increasingly irate officer. "Some people just don't know when to zip it."

"*WRAA!*" barked Chewie.

"I know they're gonna shoot us," Han snapped back as he gunned the engines. "Next time, *you* do the talking."

The *Falcon* shot forward, zooming toward the blockade. The Star Destroyer lay straight ahead, flanked by a *Gozanti*-class cruiser. Han swung around, putting them on a collision course with the smaller of the two vessels.

TURN TO PAGE 6.

BEFORE HE COULD CHANGE his mind, Han shut down the *Falcon's* primary power unit. Everything went dark. Chewie was not happy.

"Trust me, pal," said Han. "I know what I'm doing."

Han opened a comm channel to the Imperial fleet.

"We surrender!" he yelled into the microphone. "I repeat: we surrender."

He was lying, of course, gambling that the Imperials wouldn't waste laser bolts on a crippled ship.

But he was wrong. A squad of TIE fighters swept in, opening fire on the apparently incapacitated ship.

Without the protection of shields, the laser fire knocked out each of their systems. Propulsion, defense, even artificial gravity; it was all gone.

Han and Chewie would have to get really creative to get out of this one. . . .

THE END

CAN YOU GO BACK AND HELP HAN
MAKE A BETTER DECISION?
WHERE WILL THE ADVENTURE LEAD NEXT TIME?

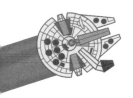

"CHEWIE, GET IN the ship, now!"

Chewbacca bared his teeth at the mob, but Han knew when they were outnumbered. He grabbed the Wookiee's arm and pulled him up the ramp.

Han just hoped that the repairs would hold. He fired the repulsors . . . and the power core blew.

The explosion ripped the *Falcon* in two! The cockpit crashed into the trees, sending Han and Chewie tumbling from their seats. Han smashed through the cracked canopy, hitting the ground hard.

As he looked up, a shadow fell across him.

It was the leader of the mob, a huge reptilian creature with four arms. Pointing his blaster down at Han, he grinned a smile worthy of a Rattataki Trogodile.

"It's about now that folk usually surrender. What d'ya say?"

THE END

CAN YOU GO BACK AND HELP HAN
MAKE A BETTER DECISION?
WHERE WILL THE ADVENTURE LEAD NEXT TIME?

NO WAY, HAN THOUGHT. *Not today. Not ever.*

He gripped the yoke with renewed vigor. "Chewie, divert everything we have to the emergency repulsors."

Chewbacca's fingers flew over the controls, and the repulsors whined as all remaining power flooded the propulsion system.

Han tested the controls. The *Falcon* responded, shifting slightly to the right. Yes, they could do this. They could take the *Falcon* down safely.

But where?

Han had only two choices: jungle or mountainside.

"What do you think, pal?" he asked Chewbacca. "Soft or hard landing—what's it gonna be?"

WHAT SHOULD HAN CHOOSE?

TO LAND THE *FALCON* IN THE JUNGLE, TURN TO PAGE 16.

TO LAND THE *FALCON* ON THE MOUNTAINSIDE, TURN TO PAGE 34.

HAN MADE A DECISION. "We need those cannons. Get the weapons back up and running, and I'll dodge the TIEs."

Big mistake. Chewie soon discovered that the *Falcon's* defensive systems were completely fried. It would take ages to repair just one of the cannons, let alone every blaster and missile launcher on the ship.

Han tried his best to evade the starfighters, but there were just too many. The *Falcon* ducked and weaved to avoid their attacks, but it was inevitable that one of the enemy pilots would eventually get lucky.

The explosion rocked the entire ship. They had no weapons and no engines. Han could only sit back as the *Falcon* was grabbed by a tractor beam. Sure, he'd find a way out of this mess, but it might take a while. . . .

THE END

**CAN YOU GO BACK AND HELP HAN
MAKE A BETTER DECISION?
WHERE WILL THE ADVENTURE LEAD NEXT TIME?**

"MY NAME'S HAN SOLO," he told them, "and I work for myself."

"Then no one will miss you," Nodo replied, grinning horribly. "Take 'em back to the yard."

Something cold clamped around Han's neck. Nearby, he heard Chewie growl.

"Get a shock collar on the Wookiee, too," Nodo ordered.

"What are you going to do to us?" Han asked, trying to pull the heavy collar from his neck.

Nodo's hand went to a control on his belt, and Han cried out as electricity arched out of the collar.

Nodo loomed over him as Han gasped for breath.

"That's what happens if you try to take off your collar. From this day on, you work for me, Han Solo, and so does your Wookiee."

THE END

CAN YOU GO BACK AND HELP HAN
MAKE A BETTER DECISION?
WHERE WILL THE ADVENTURE LEAD NEXT TIME?

"THERE'S NO WAY they'll believe we're a medical ship," Han said, broadcasting the code for the diplomatic cruiser.

There was a moment's hesitation before the controller coldly declared: *"This identification code is fake. You will surrender immediately."*

Han powered up the weapons. "So much for trusting Azmorigan. We're gonna have to blast our way through."

The *Falcon* zoomed toward the blockade. The Star Destroyer lay straight ahead, flanked by an Imperial cruiser. Han swung around, putting them on a collision course with the smaller of the two vessels.

TURN TO PAGE 6.

HAN PUSHED HIMSELF UP.

"I'll take the cannons; you get us out of here."

Chewie called after him, but Han wasn't listening. He could barely think with the pain in his shoulder, which was only made worse by the climb down to the cannons.

But Han refused to give up. No one could man the *Falcon's* guns better than he could. He knew that weapons system better than anyone.

Wincing, Han dropped into the gunner's seat and tried to lock on to the nearest starfighter.

It was impossible. His shoulder was seizing up, making it difficult to aim. He fired, but his shots went wide, missing the TIE completely.

The Imperial pilot had no such trouble. The TIE fighter blasted the *Falcon*, knocking out the already damaged engines with a single shot.

Han gripped his aching shoulder as his ship shook violently. The blockade controller's voice boomed over the comm, telling them that a shuttle was on its way and they should prepare to be boarded.

They were sunk . . . for now at least. They'd find a way to escape, but it wasn't going to be easy. Han sighed. If only he'd let Chewie man the cannons . . .

THE END

CAN YOU GO BACK AND HELP HAN
MAKE A BETTER DECISION?
WHERE WILL THE ADVENTURE LEAD NEXT TIME?

"THIS BETTER WORK," Han murmured, transmitting the code for the medical vessel.

"What was that?" asked the controller.

"Can't wait to get to work," Han lied.

"Hmmm." The Imperial officer didn't sound convinced. *"Checking now."*

The comm fell silent. Sweat prickled beneath Han's collar. If they discovered that the ID codes were fake . . .

"Everything is in order," the Imperial officer reported. *"You're free to proceed."*

"W-we are?" Han stammered, not quite believing their luck. "I mean, we are. Thanks. We'll be on our way."

"You need to fix that transmitter."

"You bet," Han said, firing up the sublight engines. "As soon as we deliver the medicine. Over and out."

The controller wasn't finished yet. *"Where are you heading?"*

The question stopped Han in his tracks. "Sorry?"

"Which planet? I originally served in the Western Reaches. On Rattatak."

Trust Han to get a chatty Imperial officer. "Oh, you

know the Western Reaches. It's a big place. Lots and lots of planets."

"*Which one?*" the controller asked again. Her tone had hardened.

"A big one. Sort of . . . greeny? With oceans . . . and trees. Lots of trees. Who doesn't like trees?" He winced. This wasn't going well. "Do you like trees?" he added weakly.

"*I like planets with names,*" the controller snapped. "*Tell me your destination, now.*"

WHAT SHOULD HAN DO?

MAKE UP A PLANET'S NAME AND HOPE FOR THE BEST—TURN TO PAGE 29. GIVE UP ON THE LIE AND TRY TO BLAST HIS WAY THROUGH THE BLOCKADE—TURN TO PAGE 43.

LIKE THE *FALCON*, Meech's speeder bike was faster than it looked. Han was impressed. It was quiet, too, the engine purring softly as he weaved in and out of the trees. As he approached the shipyard, the ground gave way to swamp. Han was sure he saw something move in the mire, but he didn't have the time or the inclination to investigate further.

The shipyard was hardly what you'd call impressive; it was just a huddle of rickety workshops in the middle of the jungle—nothing like the shipyards from Han's home planet of Corellia. Most of the buildings looked as though they'd been constructed from junked ships. There was no one to be seen. The only living souls were a scraggy flock of Lammaxian turkeys pecking noisily at the dirt.

Scrap was everywhere, from gutted transports to piles of crates and containers—perfect cover for a thief.

Han powered down the speeder, leaving it resting behind a stack of rust-covered barrels. He read the label on the nearest drum. Rhydonium—starship fuel— far cheaper than coaxium but still highly flammable and used throughout the galaxy.

"Rhydonium may not be as valuable as coaxium,"
Han muttered to himself, "but this much rhydonium
would be worth a fortune."

It wouldn't help the *Falcon* though.

Han peered around the barrels. There was a landing
bay on the other side of the yard, a number of ships
waiting to be dismantled. He was surprised to see a
TIE fighter of a model he had never seen before, with
horizontally mounted wings ending in sharp points. But
even that was nothing compared with the sleek yacht
moored next to an armored transport.

"Wow!" Han exclaimed, and for good reason. The

yacht was beautiful, with a long mirrorlike hull. It paled in comparison to some other star-yachts he had seen across the galaxy—it certainly wasn't as impressive as Dryden Vos's, of Crimson Dawn, for example—but it was still surprising to see such an elegant ship in such a rundown junkyard.

"Now *that's* traveling in style."

Glancing around to check that the coast was clear, Han ran for the polished craft and darted up the access ramp. Inside, the yacht was just as luxurious, with leather seats and gilded control panels.

Even the engine was surprisingly pristine. A smile broke across Han's face as he spotted not one but three heat exchangers, all compatible with the *Falcon's* hyperdrive.

Now he just had to remove one without being caught.

IS HAN DISCOVERED REMOVING THE PART?

YES—TURN TO PAGE 57.

NO—TURN TO PAGE 110.

REMOVING THE PART took longer than Han thought it would. He'd never seen so many bolts holding a part in place.

"Come on," he murmured as he finally eased the component from its housing. "That's it. That's . . ."

"Who are you?" said someone with a mechanical voice behind him. Han whirled around, nearly dropping the exchanger. The droid that filled the doorway was easily as big as a Gamorrean guard. Its arms were powerful pistons, and its single red eye was fixed on Han.

Usually, Han wouldn't think twice about blasting a droid, no matter how large it was, but with his hands full, there was no way to go for his gun.

"Here," he said, throwing the exchanger to the surprised robot. "Catch."

The droid obeyed, its pincers snatching the unit from the air. It was the distraction Han needed. His blaster in hand, he shot the machine in its oversize chest.

The robot toppled backward, clattering to the floor. Stepping over the deactivated droid, Han plucked the exchanger from its grasp. "Thanks. You've been a great help."

"Is that right?" came another voice. Han looked up to see an intimidating man with an overblown rifle in his slablike hands. This one was human, with skin scrawled with multiple tattoos and a nose so flat it must have been broken on numerous occasions. He wore greasy overalls complete with a patch giving what Han assumed was his name: GORKO.

"Drop it," the tattooed bruiser told him.

Han remained frozen where he stood. "What? The exchanger or the blaster?"

"Both. Nodo will want to see you."

Han had little choice but to comply. "And I want to see Nodo, whoever he is."

"You'll find out soon enough."

And find out he did. Han was led to a reptilian easily as tall as Chewie. Nodo had four powerful arms and a permanent snarl on his green-scaled face. He was wearing an oily vest and had a packed tool belt slung around his wide hips.

"Who's this?" Nodo said as he glowered at Han with snakelike eyes.

"He shot Esstee-Ninety-Three," Gorko said, his voice dripping with venom.

"Big mistake," Nodo said. "Ninety-Three was Gorko's best friend."

Han looked over his shoulder at the tattooed man's scowling face. "Then I did you a favor. Seriously, how dumb can a droid get?"

Gorko's eyes flashed with anger, but before the thug could bash Han with his blaster, Nodo cut in: "I say you're the dumb one. Who are ya?"

Han turned slowly back to the four-armed alien. He had an idea. He was pretty sure it was a terrible idea, but it was the only one he had. "You want to know my name? I'll tell you my name."

Nodo raised the boney ridges that passed for eyebrows.

"I'm waiting. . . ."

Han held his head up high. "My name is . . . Jabba the Hutt."

DOES NODO BELIEVE HAN IS JABBA?

YES—GO TO PAGE 104.
NO—GO TO PAGE 137.

"MY NAME'S HAN SOLO, and I work for Jabba the Hutt."

"Is that so? Then maybe he'll pay a ransom for your safe return."

Han snorted. "Jabba? Waste credits on *us*? Don't make me laugh."

"Only one way to find out," Nodo said, turning to his men. "Take 'em back to the yard."

He heard Chewie roar in anger, only to be silenced by a stun beam.

"And if Jabba doesn't pay?" Han asked as he was pushed toward the trees.

Nodo stopped and turned back, grinning horribly. "Then we put you to work."

Something heavy and cold was clamped around Han's neck. A shock collar. He'd be forced to work or receive an electric shock.

At least I still have Chewie, Han thought.

Han and Chewie had gotten out of a fair number of scrapes and sticky situations before. They would just have to find a way to work together to get out of this one, too.

But their new boss seemed even worse than Jabba.

As they were led through the trees, Han made himself a promise: once they escaped this joker, they'd never work for anyone else ever again.

THE END

CAN YOU GO BACK AND HELP HAN
MAKE A BETTER DECISION?
WHERE WILL THE ADVENTURE LEAD NEXT TIME?

HAN OPENED THE *FALCON'S* docking ring and looked down at the ground.

He couldn't believe it had come to this. Shifting the bulky ejector pack on his back, he stood aside so Chewie could fling himself from the plummeting craft.

Then it was Han's turn. Taking one last look at the ship he was leaving behind, Han leapt from the *Millennium Falcon* and dropped through the air.

The pack bleeped as he fell, its built-in computer calculating the perfect altitude at which to deploy. For a split second Han panicked, thinking it wasn't going to work, but then the pack activated, encasing him in a large protective sphere made of thick rubberized material.

The ball bounced as it hit the ground, shooting back into the air. Han was safely cushioned inside, or at least that was the idea.

"This. Is. Not. Fun," he complained as the ball bounced over and over again, every jolt jarring Han's already aching body. "Not. Fun. At. All!"

Finally—mercifully—the orb rolled to a stop next to Chewie's own padded sphere. The cold air of the mountainside took Han's breath away as the giant ball unzipped to release him.

Or perhaps it was the sound of a mighty explosion that thundered across the alien landscape.

The *Millennium Falcon* had crashed.

The ship that Han Solo had won in a sabacc game—the ship that made the Kessel Run in less than twelve parsecs—was now a burning heap of rubble. And Han and Chewie were stranded on a strange jungle planet. Han had no idea how they would get out of this one. . . .

THE END

CAN YOU GO BACK AND HELP HAN
MAKE A BETTER DECISION?
WHERE WILL THE ADVENTURE LEAD NEXT TIME?

HAN WASN'T ABOUT TO let a droid bully anyone.

It was an old PJ unit, mainly used in mines, like the spice mines on Kessel. He could blast it from a distance, but that would make too much noise. Instead, he crept up behind the mechanical menace and jabbed his blaster into its back panel.

"What the—"

Han fired a muffled shot and the droid fell to the ground.

He threw Meech a mock salute. "Told you we were friends. Catch you around."

Han turned to find himself staring down the barrel of a huge blaster held by an equally intimidating alien. He was almost as tall as Chewbacca, with scaly skin and four muscular arms.

"And who," the newcomer said, "are you?"

"Who am *I*?" Han repeated, feigning shock. "You don't know who I am?"

The alien snarled, revealing sharp yellow teeth. "Should I?"

"He has a ship," Meech blurted out. "In the jungle."

Han turned to glare at the woman. "So much for friendship . . ."

She gave him an apologetic shrug.

"Ah'm the only friend y'll need around here," growled the alien. "Drop the weapon."

Han did as he was told. There was no way he could shoot first, not at that range. "You don't want to do this."

"Is that right?"

"Yeah, I'm a pretty big deal."

The lizard man guffawed as aliens of all shapes and sizes emerged from the buildings carrying blasters.

"You okay, Boss?" asked a small Hoopaloo.

"'Boss'?" Han repeated, trying to remain in control of the situation. "So, you're Nodo."

The reptilian alien grinned. "Yeah, and a bigger deal than you'll ever be."

"Oh, yeah?" Han replied, thinking on his feet. "You want to know my name? I'll tell you my name."

Nodo's lips pulled back in a sneer. "Ah'm waitin'. . . ."

Han puffed out his chest and hooked his thumbs in his belt.

"The name's Hutt. Jabba the Hutt."

DOES NODO BELIEVE HAN?

YES—GO TO PAGE 104.
NO—GO TO PAGE 137.

THE LAST THING Han expected was for Nodo to shake his scaly head. "No."

"No? What do you mean? I'm Jabba the Hutt, remember?"

This time Nodo nodded. "Yeah, and there are plenty of folk in this system who don't hold with the Hutts. Powerful people. *Dangerous* people."

Nodo grabbed a blaster from his thick waist and pointed it straight at Han.

"Whoa there, what're you doing?"

"I'm sorry, Jabba. It's just not worth the risk, but handin' you over to your enemies? Well, that's different. Just imagine the bounty, especially if I blast you myself!"

TURN TO PAGE 90.

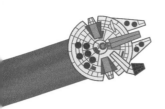

"DON'T MAKE ME REGRET THIS," Han said, clambering into the transport's cab. The engine fired on the first attempt, the vehicle rising unsteadily from the ground. Han pushed down on the accelerator and the transport jumped forward. Soon they were speeding through the smoke, engineers and Mandalorians leaping out of their way.

"How are we going to get through the trees?" Han called over his shoulder.

"I know a path through the jungle," Meech replied, and started reeling off directions.

"You sure you know where we're going?" Han said as he swerved the transport this way and that. "All these trees look alike."

Chewie bellowed a response on Meech's behalf as he brushed away the last of the foam from the hostages.

"Look," Han snapped back, "I just don't like taking orders, okay? Not from Jabba, not from you, and definitely not from—"

He broke off as he was forced to slam the thrusters in reverse. The transport jerked to a halt, throwing Meech off her feet.

She scrambled over to the cab. "So much for following my directions!"

"I *was*," Han insisted, "and look where they got us."

A steep incline rose in front of them.

"We'll never get over that," Han told her. Meech was forced to agree. To make things worse, the ground on both sides of them gave way to swamp. The decrepit transport would never make it over marsh water, either.

"We'll have to reverse out," Han said, just as they heard the telltale howl of Mandalorian rocket packs in the distance.

"They're coming after us," said Meech.

"Then we need to go over the swamp," Han said.

"No," she insisted. "We go straight ahead."

"There's a hill!"

"And this thing has laser cannons!"

Han couldn't believe what he was hearing. "You want us to *tunnel* our way to the *Falcon*?"

She held his gaze defiantly. "Unless you have a better idea."

WHAT DO THEY DO?

ESCAPE ACROSS THE SWAMP—TURN TO PAGE 105.
BLAST THROUGH THE HILL—TURN TO PAGE 123.

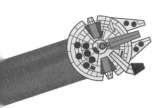

OUTSIDE, NODO GOT a nasty surprise when a heavy-duty blaster cannon dropped from the ship's undercarriage and swiveled toward them.

"Down!" he yelled as it opened fire, bolts striking at least three of his thugs.

Nodo looked up at the blaster. There was nothing he didn't know about ships and their armaments. That was an Ax-108. The thieving gully rat of a pilot obviously thought he'd been clever the day he installed it. Nodo knew differently.

"Gorko!" he yelled at a tattooed brute holding a double-barreled pulse rifle. "See the gas hose on the cannon?"

Gorko nodded.

"Light it up!"

The muscled brute fired, and the hose erupted in flames. Nodo smiled as energy flowed freely across the bottom of the ship's fuselage.

Nodo's men succeeded in blasting through the boarding ramp. They stormed the ship, finding and subduing a groggy Wookiee who had been stunned by the power backlash.

"Dangerous things, Ax-one-oh-eights," Nodo said as they found the equally dazed and confused pilot in the cockpit. "If the gas pipe ruptures it can spark a chain reaction. Most of your systems are now kaput, but don't worry, we'll still make money from this rattletrap . . . when we sell her for scrap."

THE END

HAN'S ADVENTURE IS OVER FOR NOW.
CAN YOU GO BACK AND HELP HIM
MAKE A BETTER DECISION?
WHERE WILL THE ADVENTURE LEAD NEXT TIME?

"HELP?" NODO SAID, a worried look passing over his scaled face. "Y'mean for free?"

Han waved away the question as if it were crazy. "Of course not. I'm a very rich Hutt. I'd gladly pay for your services. And then maybe arrange an exclusive contract for any future work?"

Nodo's eyes gleamed with avarice. "What kind of sum are we talkin'?"

Han plucked a figure out of the air. "Oh, I don't know. Ten, maybe twenty million . . ."

The reptilian's mouth dropped open.

Behind Han, Meech took a step forward. "But you said you didn't have—"

The rest of the woman's sentence was lost as Nodo pressed a button on his belt. Electricity coursed over Meech's arms and legs and she dropped to the floor, gasping in agony.

"Is she all right?" Han asked, concerned.

Nodo wrinkled his nose at the girl. "Meech is a cyborg, and her bionic limbs *malfunction* from time to time." He gestured for the Hoopaloo to help Meech to her feet. "Don't worry. Skreech will look after her."

The bird man scurried over to Meech and hauled her up none too kindly.

"You okay?" Han asked her.

Before she could answer, two of Nodo's arms wrapped around Han's shoulders, guiding him away.

"It's gonna be a pleasure doing business with you, Jabba. We'll get your ship up and runnin' in no time. While you wait, why don't you relax in my personal yacht." He indicated the sleek ship Han had already plundered. "You hungry? Thirsty? Anything you want, it's yours. From now on, my home is your home."

Han grinned. Maybe he was going to like it there after all.

Chewbacca did *not* like it there—not one bit. And he wasted no time in telling Han so, over and over again.

Han couldn't understand why the Wookiee was complaining. Nodo's crew had provided everything Chewbacca needed to repair the *Falcon*. Of course, Han couldn't help. He was too busy being treated like royalty on board Nodo's yacht. The food—apparently cooked by Skreech—was surprisingly good.

Admittedly, Chewie wasn't getting the same treatment. Skreech had supplied the Wookiee with a few scraps of moldy bread, thinking Chewbacca was little more than a lackey.

Han tried telling Chewie he wasn't enjoying himself, either. "We've just got to keep up the act," he said, tucking into yet another turkey drumstick. "At least until the repairs are done. As long as Nodo thinks I'm a ruthless crime lord, we're free and clear."

What no one knew was that in the shipyard's greasy kitchens, Skreech was chirping urgently into a comlink.

"That's right," he said, holding the device close to his wart-covered beak. "Nodo's doing business with *Jabba the Hutt*. He's here right now. I thought you'd want to know. . . ."

TURN TO PAGE 138.

HAN'S HEART SANK. He just couldn't do it. He couldn't fly off and leave Meech and the hostages to their fate. He wanted to. He wasn't a hero. He was a scoundrel; everyone said so. And he *liked* being a scoundrel—always had been, always would be.

But standing there, looking into Meech's eyes, he knew what he had to do.

"Chewie!" he yelled up to the TIE's cockpit. "Change of plan. We're taking the transport."

TURN TO PAGE 68.

NO, HAN TOLD HIMSELF. It would be better to bide his time, to wait until the *Falcon* was ready to fly.

He slipped the remote into a pouch on his belt. Not long now.

Or so he thought.

The sudden roar of repulsors made Han look up. A massive cruiser was descending, its red-and-yellow hull bristling with weapons. Without warning it opened fire. Han ran for the yacht, only to see a bolt of plasma blast the luxury craft into glistening shards of shrapnel.

Across the yard, Nodo bellowed, "What is the meaning of this?"

A hologram appeared in the air, projected from the spaceship. It was a Quarren, long squid-like tentacles writhing beneath her jaw.

"Lallani?" Nodo gasped. "We have no quarrel with you."

The hologram's eyes narrowed. "No, but we have a dispute with your guest."

"What guest?"

"Jabba the Hutt," Lallani announced. "I warned that

treacherous worm what would happen if he dared enter my territory."

"There's no one here by that name," Nodo claimed, but Lallani wouldn't listen.

"Bring him to me, or I'll destroy your pathetic junkyard."

Her threat delivered, Lallani's hologram promptly vanished.

Two of Nodo's men grabbed Han, dragging him over to their boss. "Hey, get off me," he said. "What are you doing?"

Nodo shrugged. "Sorry, Jabba. Ah can't afford to cross Lallani."

Han struggled but couldn't break free of his captors' grip.

"HRRRRAHH!"

Han almost cheered when he heard Chewie's roar. He twisted around to see the Wookiee racing toward them, bowcaster in hand. He must have heard the explosion and come running.

"Now you're in for it." Han grinned.

Chewie raised his bowcaster . . . and was swamped by a flood of sticky foam. Skreech had appeared in front of the Wookiee, dousing Chewbacca with filla-foam from the container on his feathered back.

Chewie was so tall that the foam only reached his chest, but it still hardened in seconds. Chewbacca was rooted to the spot, his arms and legs stuck fast in the concrete-like material. He twisted and roared but could barely move a muscle.

Lallani's voice boomed from the spaceship. *"You're running out of time, Nodo. Bring me Jabba the Hutt!"*

DOES HAN ADMIT THAT HE'S NOT REALLY JABBA?

YES—TURN TO PAGE 112.
NO—TURN TO PAGE 101.

"YOU BET I AM," Han said, turning to the hostages. "Time to earn your passage. Everyone grab a barrel."

There was much grumbling, but before long the members of Han's party were rolling the heavy drums toward the *Falcon*, Chewbacca carrying a barrel beneath each of his long arms.

The Wookiee gave Han a withering look.

Stealing starship fuel seemed to have become a hobby of theirs.

"At least it's easier this time around," Han suggested, interpreting the Wookiee's expression.

Soon cargo and passengers were stowed safely on board and Han was back in the *Falcon*'s cockpit where he belonged.

"Not a bad job," he told Chewbacca as the engine revved to life. "Couldn't have done better myself."

Before Chewie could respond, Meech appeared behind them.

"There's movement in the jungle," she told them. "I think it's Nodo."

The sudden thud of blaster fire against the hull confirmed her story.

Han flicked a switch and the display monitor showed a picture of the mechanic desperately trying to shoot his way on to the ship.

"Well, he doesn't look too happy," Han said.

Meech laughed. "Can you blame him? Losing your prisoners and your business in one day? That's gotta hurt."

"Yeah," Han agreed, grinning as he pulled back on the throttle. "Couldn't happen to a nicer guy."

Outside, Nodo was blown off his feet as the *Millennium Falcon*'s powerful engines propelled the ship high into the sky.

"Just wait till I find you, you no-good faker!" he yelled, shaking three of his fists at the disappearing cruiser. "You made an enemy today. Do y'hear? A dangerous enemy!"

Of course, Han couldn't hear a word. And he was busy planning his next move.

"Plot a course to the nearest spaceport," he instructed Chewie as soon as they were clear of the planet's atmosphere.

Behind him, Meech frowned. "And then what?"

"Then we say good-bye."

"That's it? You just dump us and run?"

Han raised his gloved hands from the controls.

"Hey, I got you away from Nodo, didn't I? Now you can look after yourself. Besides, I've got rhydonium to sell. Need to pay Jabba off somehow."

Chewbacca looked back at Meech's downhearted expression and rumbled a response to Han.

"Give the fuel to *her*?" Han raised a finger to shut up the Wookiee. "No. Not happening. Not in a million years."

"It would help me get the hostages home," Meech pointed out.

Han turned to look at her. "And why should I? You've been nothing but trouble. The first time we met, you even tried to shoot me!"

"Because I was going to steal your ship to escape."

"And now you've escaped. Thanks to me."

This time, Chewbacca didn't growl; he just cocked his head and looked at Han with soulful eyes.

"You're not guilting me into this," the smuggler told the Wookiee. "That fuel is ours, fair and square."

DOES HAN GIVE THE FUEL TO MEECH?

YES—TURN TO PAGE 92.
NO—TURN TO PAGE 96.

WITHIN MINUTES, the *Falcon* was back where she belonged, in open space.

"Time to face the music," Han said as Chewie set course for Tatooine. "Maybe Jabba won't be *too* upset about his cargo."

Han pumped the hyperdrive and the *Falcon* spluttered, smoke billowing from the back of the ship. The thrum of the engines promptly died and they were afloat, without engines or thrusters.

He was forced to send out a distress signal, which was soon answered. A shrill voice burbled over the comm: *"Hello? Who is this?"*

Han's heart sank. He recognized that voice.

"Azmorigan. It's me—Han. We're in a tight spot over here."

His next question stuck in his craw.

"Any chance you could, er, rescue us?"

On the other end of the comm, Azmorigan dissolved into gleeful laughter.

"Me? Rescue you? Ha-ha-ha-ha! This'll cost you, Solo. This will cost you big!"

Han couldn't believe it. If he survived making a deal with the Jablogian, maybe he should finally quit smuggling and take up something less dangerous.

Like rathtar wrestling . . .

THE END

**CAN YOU GO BACK AND HELP HAN
MAKE A BETTER DECISION?
WHERE WILL THE ADVENTURE LEAD NEXT TIME?**

HAN STILL WOULDN'T LISTEN. Wrestling with the controls, he tried to fly the TIE fighter toward the *Falcon*.

Unfortunately, Lallani had a different idea.

The first blast struck them from behind, bursting through the hull. Chewie looked through the smoking hole to spy a group of Mandalorians flying toward them using rocket packs.

"You've gotta be kidding me," Han snarled. "How many?"

"*HRUAAA!*"

"Three?" Han repeated. "Next you'll be telling me they can fly straight."

Han knew they were in trouble. It was all he could do to keep the starfighter on course, and TIEs had no rear armaments. Chewie had dropped his trusty bowcaster in the skirmish on the ground. They were defenseless.

He swung the fighter from side to side. A moving target was more difficult to hit, not that the Mandalorians seemed to be having much trouble. Disintegrator fire peppered the cockpit, hitting the

starfighter's laser bank. It exploded, sending the tiny craft spinning out of control.

The starfighter crashed through the trees, its wings ripped away by grasping branches. They only stopped when the cockpit got ensnared in a web of tangled vines. Han and Chewie hung helplessly, the cockpit swinging like a pendulum, as the hovering Mandalorians called for their surrender.

Han raised his hands.

Sure, they were hideously outgunned and kilometers away from their ship . . . but that had never stopped Han and Chewie before. . . .

THE END

CAN YOU GO BACK AND HELP HAN
MAKE A BETTER DECISION?
WHERE WILL THE ADVENTURE LEAD NEXT TIME?

HAN'S HAND WENT TO his sonic spanner. It was worth a try. He thumbed the control, the tool vibrating in his palm. He'd once seen a singer shatter a bottle of jogan fruit juice by hitting a high note. If he could find the right frequency, maybe he could crack the foam that covered most of Chewie's body.

He pressed the tool against the Wookiee's encased chest.

"MWRAAAA," Chewie complained, saying that the vibration was giving him a headache.

"You're not the only one," said someone with a silky voice. Han turned to see Lallani standing behind him, her electro-whip buzzing at her side. "So, you're the one who claimed to be Jabba the Hutt?"

"Who, me?" said Han, gesturing with the spanner. "I'm just a humble mechanic. No one special at all."

Lallani cracked her whip, knocking the spanner from Han's grasp. Electric current surged up his arm, knocking him back into Chewbacca's immobile body. He slid to the ground, cradling his stinging fingers.

Two of Lallani's mercenaries stomped up. Slapping binders on his wrists, they dragged him back to his feet.

"You're a terrible liar but will make a wonderful slave," Lallani purred. "As will your little pet."

Han was marched to her ship and thrown into a cramped cell. A minute later Chewie was tossed in with him, the Wookiee's arms and legs still stuck fast in the filla-foam.

"Don't worry, pal," Han said as the door to their prison slid shut, "we'll get out of this in no time. It'll be like on Mimban. We just have to figure out how. . . ."

THE END

CAN YOU GO BACK AND HELP HAN
MAKE A BETTER DECISION?
WHERE WILL THE ADVENTURE LEAD NEXT TIME?

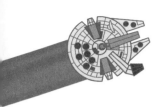

THE REPTILIAN DIDN'T GET a chance to fire. Plasma bolts streaked across the shipyard, igniting a nearby stack of rhydonium barrels.

The blast threw Han from his feet, and when he looked up, he saw Chewbacca striding through the smoke, bowcaster blazing.

Chewie must have followed from the *Falcon*!

That Wookiee never lets me down, Han thought.

He made a mental note to thank Chewie later for saving his skin.

"This way," Han said, snatching his own blaster from the ground.

They ran for the speeder, Han taking the controls while Chewie sat behind, firing round after round from his bowcaster.

They streaked out of the shipyard, heading back to the *Falcon*.

"*HRRRAA!*" Chewie bellowed over a hairy shoulder.

"The heat exchanger?" Han answered. "Yeah, had a little trouble with that. Don't worry. We'll still be able to take off."

Chewie didn't sound convinced, even when they got back to the ship and Han devised a lash-up that bypassed the heat exchangers completely.

"She'll hold together," Han told him as he punched the engines. "Trust me."

With a roar like a wounded animal, the *Millennium Falcon* soared into the sky.

TURN TO PAGE 83.

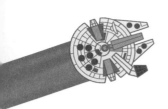

"I CAN'T BELIEVE you guilted me into that," said Han as they blasted away from the spaceport. Despite Han's better judgment, they had left the fuel with Meech and the hostages.

Chewbacca chuckled, looking pleased with himself.

Han shook his head. He knew they'd done the right thing, but it also left them with a problem.

"You know Jabba's gonna be furious, don't you? We'll have to pay him double to make up for this."

Chewie's smile faded.

"Or we'll be on the run, hunted by Jabba's goons wherever we go."

This time Chewbacca didn't reply. He just looked at Han, who was grinning from ear to ear.

"But what else is new? He'll have to catch us first."

With that, Han Solo pulled back on the hyperdrive lever, and the *Millennium Falcon* shot into the stars.

THE END

**CONGRATULATIONS! YOU HELPED HAN AND CHEWIE
MAKE IT THROUGH THEIR LATEST ADVENTURE!**

"HRAAA!" CHEWIE BAWLED as Han bundled the Wookiee back into the *Falcon*.

"Yeah, I know what you said about the power core," Han told him as they charged into the cockpit. "I just hoped you were exaggerating."

Han pressed the controls, but nothing happened. The *Falcon* was still grounded.

He turned to Chewbacca. "What if we reroute power through the secondary cooling system? Would that work?"

Chewie shook his head.

"Can we try anyway?"

Rolling his eyes, Chewie rushed into the bowels of the ship. Outside, Nodo's mob was desperately trying to blast their way through the closed ramp.

"We'll see about that," Han said, reaching for the control that activated the blaster cannon hidden in the *Falcon*'s belly.

DOES THE BLASTER CANNON WORK?

YES—GO TO PAGE 70.

NO—GO TO PAGE 135.

THE EGGS' SPICY AROMA was making Han's mouth water. He gobbled down one, and then another and another.

He didn't even notice that Meech had gone. All he cared about was the eggs. He wasn't even that hungry, but soon the platter was empty.

"Enjoyed your supper?" chirped a voice from the door.

It was Skreech, the bird man.

"Compliments to the chef," Han said, his mouth full. "I couldn't stop myself."

Skreech smirked. "That'll be my special secret ingredient. Makes them impossible to resist."

But Han was struggling to focus on Skreech's words. In fact, he was struggling to stand. His legs buckled beneath him and he crashed to the floor. Skreech appeared above him, cocking his head like an Endorian chicken.

"What's wrong with me?" Han slurred.

"That'll be the *other* secret ingredient," Skreech replied, "the one that relaxes you just long enough for me to deliver you into the hands of your enemies."

Han was unable to move. "My . . . what?"

"There are plenty of folk around here who don't like you, Jabba. Folk willing to offer a bounty on your head."

Han wanted to tell the bird man that he wasn't Jabba, that it had all been a lie, but he could no longer speak. He was helpless and at the Hoopaloo's mercy. Where was Chewie when Han needed him?

THE END

CAN YOU GO BACK AND HELP HAN
MAKE A BETTER DECISION?
WHERE WILL THE ADVENTURE LEAD NEXT TIME?

JUST A FEW HOURS LATER, Han flopped back into the pilot's chair and plotted a course for Tatooine.

He was happy. They'd deposited Meech and the hostages on the first space station they'd found and were back on their way.

Chewbacca, however, was still sulking.

On the dashboard, a comm light started winking. Han opened the channel, knowing exactly whose voice he'd hear.

"Solo," boomed Jabba in Huttese. *"Where is my cargo?"*

Han swallowed and told the crime lord how they'd been forced to dump the stolen tech at an Imperial checkpoint.

"What?" Jabba thundered. *"I'll have your head for this, Solo!"*

Han raised a calming hand, even though their disgruntled employer couldn't see. "Jabba, it's fine. I have a shipment of rhydonium in the hold, more than enough to cover the cost."

"Rhydonium?" Jabba shouted. *"Why would I need rhydonium? I have drilling platforms on Abafar,*

Tralgaria, and Saracor. I sell rhydonium to space wasters, not the other way around. Just wait till I get my hands on you, Solo. I'll feed you to the sandswimmers. I'll blast you into the suns of Arkanis. I'll—"

Han clicked off the comm and sat staring at the stars. He could feel Chewie's eyes on him.

"You're gonna tell me we could have given the fuel to Meech, aren't you?"

The Wookiee didn't reply. He didn't have to. Han already knew he'd messed up. Jabba wasn't going to forgive him, not this time.

THE END

CAN YOU GO BACK AND HELP HAN
MAKE A BETTER DECISION?
WHERE WILL THE ADVENTURE LEAD NEXT TIME?

"NO," HAN SAID, desperately trying to keep the starfighter in the air. "We made our decision, and now we have to stick with it."

He glanced down at the ground. The shipyard was a mess, smoke rising from a dozen fires. The battle belonged to Lallani. Her Mandalorians were swarming toward the transport. Was Meech still inside, trying to free the hostages?

She'd never make it . . . not unless she had some help.

"Ah, who am I kidding?" Han said, pushing down on the controls. "Who wants to fly one of these things anyway?"

On the ground, Lallani's guards looked up to see a sharp-winged TIE fighter plunging toward them. They scattered as the stricken craft struck the ground, its wings snapping off to leave the lozenge-shaped hull rolling like a hyper-bowl ball.

Chewbacca kicked out the circular viewport when the steaming wreck eventually came to a rest. Han jumped down, followed by the Wookiee, as disintegrator blasts pummeled the downed starfighter, the Mandalorians realizing that Han and his copilot had survived the crash.

"Over here!" Meech shouted from the transport, and returning fire, Han raced for the armored vehicle.

Meech grinned as they ducked through the door. "You came back."

"Didn't have much choice," Han claimed, although he was smiling, too. "How you getting on with those hostages?"

"Slowly," Meech admitted.

Han made for the transport's controls. "Lend her a hand, Chewie. I'm gonna get this thing moving."

GO TO PAGE 68.

"SORRY, KID. You're on your own."

Han wasn't a hero—never had been, never would be.

He clambered up to the starfighter's hatch and swung himself into the cockpit. Unlike standard TIE fighters, this one had space for a crew of two. Chewie was already priming the starfighter's thrust generator, but he was brooding, avoiding Han's eyes.

Han ignored him and pulled back on the control stem. With a demented howl, the fighter shot into the air.

But the bizarre TIE was impossible to fly. Its stabilizers were hopelessly misaligned, the tiny ship incapable of flying straight.

As Han struggled with the controls, Chewie reminded him they should've helped the hostages. If they'd taken the ground transport they wouldn't be in this mess.

"You think I don't know that?"

Chewbacca told him they still had time to go back.

DOES HAN LISTEN TO CHEWIE?

YES—TURN TO PAGE 98.
NO—TURN TO PAGE 85.

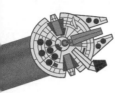

"SORRY, PAL," NODO SAID to Han. "It's either you or me . . . and I like me more."

"The feeling ain't mutual," Han growled, but there was little he could do.

"We have him," Nodo called into the air. "We have Jabba."

In response, Lallani's ship landed in front of them, its repulsors throwing up clouds of dust. Han was still spluttering as Lallani swept down the ramp dressed in long red robes, holding a coiled electro-whip. She was flanked by two armor-clad Mandalorian mercenaries, both carrying disintegrators.

Lallani looked at Han and then back at Nodo. "Well? Where is Jabba?"

Nodo pointed at Han. "He's right here."

Lallani laughed. "This puny creature? He's not Jabba the Hutt."

"Who are you calling puny?" Han shot back, ignoring the shocked look on Nodo's face.

"B-but," Nodo stammered, "he said—"

"Enough," Lallani interrupted, silencing him with a crack of her whip. "I have no time for your deceit.

Guards, show them what happens to people who waste my time."

The Mandalorians zapped the nearest stack of rhydonium with their disintegrators. The barrels exploded, setting off a chain reaction across the shipyard.

Han's captors let go of his arms as thick smoke billowed through the base. This was his chance to escape, but he couldn't leave Nodo's hostages to their fate. Lallani was mad enough to blow up the entire base.

Running for Chewbacca, Han snatched Nodo's remote from the pouch on his belt and thumbed the master control. On the other side of the shipyard, the transport's doors opened.

But what could he do about Chewie? His friend was still trapped from the chest down in foam.

Or was he? Cracks were appearing as Chewbacca strained beneath the hardened material. It was the heat from the flaming barrels. It was melting the foam.

"Hang in there, buddy," Han said, trying to pry the cracks apart. "We'll get you out of there."

HOW CAN HAN GET CHEWIE OUT OF THE FOAM?

USE A WELDER—TURN TO PAGE 127.

USE A HAMMER—TURN TO PAGE 134.

USE A SPANNER—TURN TO PAGE 88.

HAN HELD HIS BREATH. He had no idea if his gamble would pay off. These crooks might not even know who Jabba was. And if they did, would they realize that Han looked absolutely nothing like a Hutt?

Nodo dropped into a respectful, if nervous, bow.

"J-Jabba," he stammered. "It's an honor to welcome you to my humble yard. If ah'd known it was you . . ."

Han had to stop himself from laughing out loud. They'd bought it!

"I will forgive you, just this once."

The reptilian looked relieved, but Han piled on the pressure.

"Your friend is right. I do have a ship in the jungle. We ran into a little Imperial trouble and were forced to crash a kilometer or so from here. My . . . er . . . *associate* is making repairs." Han looked around at Nodo's gang of reprobates. "Perhaps you could help?"

WILL NODO'S GANG HELP FIX THE *MILLENNIUM FALCON*?

YES—TURN TO PAGE 72.

NO—TURN TO PAGE 67.

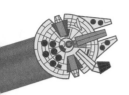

"JUST WATCH ME," Han said, reversing the carrier out over the swamp.

"What are you doing?" Meech cried. "The repulsors will never make it across marsh water. They need solid ground."

"You'll be amazed at what repulsors can do. And what I can do, for that matter."

The carrier skidded across the swamp, sending up plumes of murky water on either side.

"You know, this might just work," Han exclaimed as they bounced over a small island in the bog.

"'Might'?" Meech spluttered. "I thought you were sure about it?"

"As sure as I ever get," Han said as the carrier tilted alarmingly. The cab dipped into the water and never came back out.

Han pulled hard on the controls. "No, no, no. Don't do this!"

"Don't do what?" Meech asked, hanging on to the back of his seat.

"The repulsors are flooded. We're going in."

"What did I tell you?" Meech cried as the transport slewed into the swamp with an almighty splash.

"*WRAAAAA!*" Chewie wailed from the back.

"Yes, I know we're sinking!" Han yelled. "Get everyone out."

Meech scrambled through the cab window. "What are we going to do?"

"Swim," Han said, plunging into the water. It was thick with algae and tasted like three-week-old nerf chowder. "Get to the island."

Beside him, one of the hostages yelped and disappeared beneath the surface. Then Meech vanished only to reappear seconds later, gasping for breath.

"There's something in the water," she croaked. "It grabbed my leg."

"What kind of something?"

His answer came when a tentacle as thick as Chewie's arm burst from the swamp to wrap around his chest and pull him beneath the water. He struggled against whatever monstrosity had dragged him down, but he couldn't get free. His lungs felt like they were going to burst when Chewie's giant hand plunged down and pulled him back up by his shirt.

He broke the surface, coughing up marsh water, but

the tentacle had come with him and was squeezing him tighter and tighter.

With the sudden crack of an electro-whip, the tentacle was sliced in two. The halves tumbled back into the water, the submerged predator fleeing with a muffled howl.

Coughing, Han looked up at Lallani, who sat above them on a speeder bike, electro-whip in hand. Her gang of Mandalorians hovered around her, their jet packs thundering and disintegrators ready to fire.

There was nowhere else to run. It was either surrender to Lallani or take their chances with the swamp monster that was sure to return.

Han didn't know which he'd rather face. . . .

THE END

**CAN YOU GO BACK AND HELP HAN
MAKE A BETTER DECISION?
WHERE WILL THE ADVENTURE LEAD NEXT TIME?**

"COME ON, CHEWIE," Han said, racing for the TIE.

"Wait!" Meech called after them. "How will we all fit in there?"

Chewie was already climbing up to the starfighter's hatch when Han turned to face her. "We won't. There's barely enough room for two. You guys will have to fend for yourselves."

"But you can't just leave us here," she pleaded. "*Please.*"

DOES HAN CHANGE HIS MIND?

YES—TURN TO PAGE 75.

NO—TURN TO PAGE 100.

"THAT'S IT," HAN WHISPERED as he lifted one of the exchangers from its housing. "Come to Papa."

Removing the part had taken longer than he'd expected, but his luck had held and he hadn't been discovered as he worked. Hanging the exchanger from his belt, Han made his way out of the yacht and snuck across the base. He was almost back to the speeder when he heard a voice he recognized.

"Just listen, will you?"

It was Meech. She must have escaped.

Han peered around the side of a ramshackle hut. Across the yard, the leather-clad woman was being threatened by a hulking droid.

"There's a ship, out in the jungle," she was saying, but the droid wasn't taking her seriously.

"A likely story," it said, clamping a giant pincer around Meech's forearm. "You were trying to escape. Just wait until Nodo hears about this."

DOES HAN TRY TO RESCUE MEECH?

YES—TURN TO PAGE 64.
NO, HE SHOULDN'T GET INVOLVED—TURN TO PAGE 119.

"WAIT," SAID HAN as Nodo's goons dragged him toward the ship. "You don't understand. This isn't right."

Nodo shrugged. "I like you, Jabba. You're a man after my own heart, but hey, what can a guy do? Lallani won't rest until she has you in her clutches."

"She won't rest until she has *Jabba*," Han argued. "But that's not me. I lied. I'm not Jabba the Hutt. I'm not *any* kind of Hutt."

Nodo's skin flushed beneath his scales.

"You're just saying that to save your skin!"

"No, it's true," Han replied. "My name is Han. Han Solo."

"What? I trusted you!" Nodo bellowed. "I even helped you fix yer no-good ship!"

Han tried to wriggle out of his captors' grip. "You can insult me, but leave the *Falcon* out of it. Come on, Nodo . . . what about honor among thieves? How's about you let me go?"

"Let you go? Why should I? Do you even *know* Jabba the Hutt?"

"Know Jabba? Sure I do. We're like family."

"Family?"

Han shrugged. "Distant family. Second cousins, twice removed."

Nodo's hand dropped to his blaster. Han started talking for his life. "Look, I work for him. The deals we were talking about, they could still happen. Jabba listens to me. I could persuade him to go into business with you. What d'ya say?"

In answer, Nodo turned back to the ship and called for Lallani. The woman's hologram reappeared in the air.

"Have you brought me Jabba?"

"Can't do that," Nodo told her. "This lousy junk weevil lied to me, told me he was Jabba."

"And you believed him?"

"Yes."

"Then you are a fool."

"I am, great Lallani, but I offer him to you anyway."

Han's eyes went wide. "You do?"

Lallani didn't sound impressed. "Why would I want him?"

"Because he works for Jabba. He'll have information you can use against your enemy."

"No, I won't!" Han shouted into the air. "I know nothing. Less than nothing. I'm no good at all."

Han felt static wash over his body. Nodo's men released their grip, but he still couldn't move.

"You are trapped in a localized force field," Lallani's hologram told him. "There is no escape. You and your Wookiee will be brought on board my ship, and then you will tell me everything you know about Jabba the Hutt."

From the corner of his eye, Han could see Chewie, still encased in the foam.

"Don't worry, pal," he said as Lallani's ship prepared to land. "We'll get out of this. Maybe Jabba will rescue us himself?"

They both knew that was the biggest lie of all.

THE END

CAN YOU GO BACK AND HELP HAN
MAKE A BETTER DECISION?
WHERE WILL THE ADVENTURE LEAD NEXT TIME?

NO, HE HAD EATEN ENOUGH. "Meech, wait. . . ."

She paused at the door and looked back. "What?"

He took a step closer. "It's just . . . well, you don't seem to fit in around here."

"And you don't seem to have a long tail or eat gorgs." Han winced. "So, you know, huh?"

"That you're not who you say you are?" She laughed bitterly. "Don't worry, your secret's safe with me. Not that anyone would listen anyway."

He took another step toward her. "Look, when your bionic limbs malfunctioned . . . that was no accident, was it? Nodo did it to you."

She shifted uncomfortably, putting her hands in her back pockets. This was obviously difficult for her.

"I crashed here," she explained, "four years ago. Nodo fixed my robotic arms and legs. Like you, I didn't have any credits, but unlike you, I didn't pretend to be a gangster."

"So Nodo made you work off your debt."

She laughed. "And then some." Rolling up her sleeve, Meech showed him her bionic arm. "He implanted devices that shock me every time I refuse to do as he says. That day, I became his slave."

Han was appalled. He'd guessed that Nodo was a creep, but this was a step too far.

Meech noted the expression on his face. "Think that's bad?"

She led him out of the yacht and toward the old armored transport. "Look inside."

Han peered through the window and saw men and women standing against the wall. No, they weren't standing, they were *stuck* to the wall by some kind of gloop.

"That's filla-foam, isn't it?"

Meech nodded. "Used to plug hull breaches on ships. One spray and it hardens in seconds."

"And Nodo is using it to trap *people*? Who are they?"

"Crews brought in by pirates. Nodo holds them here for ransom."

Han felt his stomach knot. He'd done plenty of dodgy stuff over the years and dealt with a lot of bad people—from the White Worms to Crimson Dawn—but this was more than just dodgy. This was downright wrong.

"Anythin' wrong?" rumbled a deep voice behind them. It was Nodo, two of his arms crossed in front of his barrel chest.

"Er, no. Meech was just showing me around," Han said.

One of Nodo's hand went down to a remote on his belt. "Was she now?"

Han raised his hands to stop him. "Because I asked her to. You did say your home was my home."

Nodo peered at the two of them for a moment before his expression softened. He laughed, strolling over to the window. "So what do you think of my little business venture?"

Han struggled to hide his disgust. "It's very . . . enterprising. Aren't you worried they'll escape?"

"Through all that foam?" Nodo slapped the transport's door. "Besides, this baby is locked up tight. Ah'm the only one with the key."

Nodo patted the remote on his belt, the same one Han suspected had caused Meech so much pain. It must also control the transport's door.

"Want in on the deal?"

He really had fallen for Han's lie. Han made a show of clapping Nodo on his broad back. "Perhaps we should discuss it over dinner?"

Nodo's face lit up. "An excellent idea. Meech, get Skreech to rustle up somethin' extra special tonight."

The cyborg glared at him. "Of course. Whatever you say, *Boss*."

"Then what're you waitin' for?" Nodo asked, waving her away.

Meech hurried off, and Nodo rubbed both sets of hands together in anticipation. "So, until tonight . . ."

"Until tonight." Han gave Nodo a thumbs up. "We can talk about that deal."

Nodo followed Meech over to the main building, obviously imagining the riches the new deal would bring. He was going to be disappointed.

"Couldn't happen to a nicer fella," Han said, looking at the remote he'd lifted from Nodo's belt. His thumb hovered over the control. With one press, Han could release Nodo's prisoners, and Meech, too.

DOES HAN RELEASE THE PRISONERS RIGHT AWAY?

YES—TURN TO PAGE 121.

NO—TURN TO PAGE 76.

HAN NEARLY INTERVENED. He wanted to, and he knew he probably should, but rescuing Meech would only get him captured, or maybe worse.

"Sorry, sister," he muttered under his breath, and made for the speeder bike. Clipping the heat exchanger to his belt, he grabbed the speeder's handlebars and crept the bike out of the camp. Quiet though it was, he couldn't risk the speeder's engine being heard.

When he was sure he was at a safe distance, Han jumped into the saddle and opened the throttle. The speeder bike streaked back to the *Falcon*, Han losing his way only once. Okay, maybe it was twice. Either way, he was soon handing the exchanger over to a grateful Chewie.

"I think that's mine," said someone behind them.

They turned to see a tall alien with two sets of powerful arms glowering at them. He was flanked by half a dozen men and women, all carrying heavy blasters.

"Don't think so, pal," Han replied. "I don't even know who you are. . . ."

"Name's Nodo." The scaly brute pointed at the heat exchanger. "And *that* came from my yacht."

Han never took his eyes off the thug. "Chewie? Reckon we can take off without the heat exchanger?"

Chewie grumbled that they could if they wanted the power core to explode as soon as they achieved orbit. Han gambled that the multiarmed alien didn't speak Wookiee. "Then give the nice slimeball his exchanger."

"Who you calling a slimeball?" Nodo snarled.

Before Han could answer, Chewie drew back his arm and threw the exchanger straight at Nodo. It smacked the alien between his snakelike eyes, and he went down hard.

It was the distraction Han needed. He aimed his blaster and fired a stun bolt, finally answering the question: "Who d'ya think?"

WHAT SHOULD HAN AND CHEWIE DO?

STAY AND FIGHT—GO TO PAGE 133.
ESCAPE IN THE *FALCON*—GO TO PAGE 93.

"THERE'S NO TIME LIKE the present," Han said, pushing the button. He heard the clunk of the transport's doors unlocking. Han also heard Skreech's cry, the scrawny bird man raising the alarm.

Nodo darted back into the yard, a blaster already in his hand. Han glanced at the transport. Where were the prisoners? Why weren't they streaming from the vehicle?

Then he realized. The filla-foam! The prisoners couldn't escape, even if they wanted to.

Nodo's stun beam struck his wounded shoulder, sending him spinning to the ground. The reptilian loomed over Han as he tried to stand on legs that were like spice jelly.

"You're no Hutt," Nodo growled. "Why would Jabba care about a few lousy hostages?"

Han couldn't answer or fight back as Nodo dragged him to the transport.

"You can stay here until we figure out what to do with you," the scaly alien said as he shoved Han through the door. Still affected by Nodo's stun beam, Han could only groan as Nodo picked up a hose and doused him in liquid filla-foam. The sticky gloop hardened within seconds, fixing Han to the wall like the other hostages.

He tried to cry out when he heard Chewie calling his name, but Nodo slapped a sweaty palm over Han's mouth, silencing him. He struggled but could only watch helplessly as Chewbacca stepped inside the transport and was trapped by another blast of Nodo's foam gun.

"MRRRAHH!" Chewie roared, struggling against the grip of the hardened gunk. Nodo laughed and stomped out of the transport, slamming the door behind him.

"Don't worry, pal," Han told his friend. "We'll think of a way out of this, one way or another. We just need a little time, that's all."

And locked inside the dusty transport, they had all the time they needed. . . .

THE END

CAN YOU GO BACK AND HELP HAN
MAKE A BETTER DECISION?
WHERE WILL THE ADVENTURE LEAD NEXT TIME?

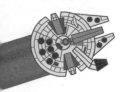

CHEWIE BELLOWED a warning from the back of the carrier. The roar from the pursuing Mandalorians was getting closer.

"Well?" Meech prompted.

"This'll never work," Han said, activating the weapons system. The transport shook as the cannon pummeled the hillside, sending clumps of dirt high in the air.

"It is!" Meech cheered. "It's working!"

"Told you it would," Han said, slamming the transport forward. They plunged into the freshly carved tunnel, the path ahead illuminated by the flickering light of their cannon fire. The noise from the blasts was almost unbearable, but at least it masked the scrape of the transport's doors against the narrow tunnel walls.

"They've found us!" Meech called out, struggling to make herself heard over the racket.

Han glanced over his shoulder. A group of Mandalorians had barreled into the tunnel, following a low-slung speeder bike.

"It's Lallani," he said, spotting the glowing whip

looped around the speeder's handles. "Charge up the rear cannon."

Meech checked the controls. "We don't have one."

"Sure we do. Chewie?"

Chewbacca was already hanging out the back door, bowcaster primed and ready. He took aim and fired. The bolt struck the scorched dirt directly above the Mandalorians. With the sound of rolling thunder, the tunnel collapsed on top of Lallani, trapping the Quarren and her mercenaries.

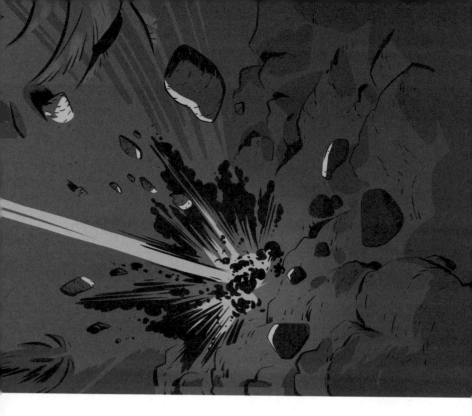

Meech clapped her hands. "Yes!"

"Don't celebrate yet," Han told her as the cannons stuttered. "Our batteries are draining fast."

Meech looked back at the collapsed tunnel behind them. "But if they fail . . ."

"We'll be buried alive," Han confirmed, flooring the accelerator. "But I'm not about to let that happen!"

With an almighty *THOOM*, the transport blasted through the other side of the hill. The repulsors burned out, and the wrecked vehicle bounced once before careening into a large purple tree.

"You did it!" Meech said, throwing her arms around Han.

"Course I did," he replied, trying to pry himself free from the hug.

"HRRRUH!" Chewie bellowed as he ushered the freed hostages from the transport.

"No need to get jealous," Han told him, jumping from the cab. "How far to the *Falcon*?"

Chewie pointed ahead, and Han turned to see the welcome sight of his ship through the trees.

"There she is," Han said, rushing ahead before stopping beside a rundown bunker that had been half buried by the undergrowth. He swung open the door to find it was filled with familiar barrels.

"More rhydonium."

Meech walked up beside him. "Nodo has stockpiles all over the jungle." Then she noticed the look on Han's face. "Wait. You're not thinking of taking them, are you?"

DOES HAN TAKE THE FUEL?

YES—TURN TO PAGE 79.
NO—TURN TO PAGE 131.

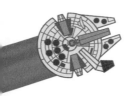

CHEWIE'S EYES went wide as Han grabbed a fusion welder from his belt.

"Don't sweat it, pal," Han said, adjusting the welder's controls. "We just need to turn up the heat."

He touched the tiny flame to the foam, which started to bubble.

Chewie's roar was getting more frantic by the second.

"Stop complaining, will you?" Han told him. "I'm not going to burn you! I'm nearly through."

Suddenly, a rough hand grabbed Han's shoulder and sent him spinning to the ground. It was Nodo, his scaly face flushed with blind fury.

"Liar!"

Han tried to scramble up, but Nodo grabbed him by his jacket and dragged him over to Lallani.

"Tell her," the reptilian barked, throwing Han at her feet. "Tell her how you lied to me!"

Han looked up at Lallani. "I may have stretched the truth. I'm not Jabba. I just work for him."

Furious that her prize had been denied her, Lallani raised her arm, the electro-whip sparking in the air.

Han screwed up his eyes, waiting for the energy flail to crack several of his bones, but the only crack was the sound of splintering filla-foam.

"*YRRRRAAAAH!*" Chewie bellowed as he broke free of his shell and grabbed a startled Nodo. Still roaring, the Wookiee lifted the mechanic high above his shaggy head and tossed him at Lallani, sending them both to the ground.

"Good work, pal," said Han as Chewie scooped him up. "Is the *Falcon* fixed?"

Chewie nodded.

"Then what are we waiting for?"

Nodo and Lallani's forces were still fighting as Han led Chewie back to the landing bay. The only surviving ships were the strange TIE fighter and the armored transport. The transport's door was open and Han could see Meech trying to free the prisoners from the filla-foam.

"Here," he said, throwing her the fusion welder. "You can burn 'em out."

"What about you?" she asked, catching the tool.

"We're heading back to our ship."

Meech rushed to the open door. "Take us with you."

Han glanced at the cocooned prisoners. "We can't wait for you to free them."

She slapped the side of the transport. "Then take

this thing. Chewie can help break them out while you drive."

Han wasn't sure. He glanced at the TIE fighter. Even if they could get the transport moving, it would be a lot slower than the starfighter.

Reluctantly, Han made his decision.

WHICH SHIP DO THEY USE TO GET BACK TO THE *FALCON*?

THE TIE FIGHTER—TURN TO PAGE 109.

THE TROOP TRANSPORT—TURN TO PAGE 68.

MEECH GRABBED HAN'S ARM and pulled him in the direction of the *Falcon*. "We don't have time, okay?"

"But . . ."

"But nothing. Stop thinking like a thief, and get us out of here!"

Chewie rumbled his agreement, and Han had little choice but to give in.

Before long, everyone was back on the ship, Meech and the hostages sheltering in one of the holds.

"Time to put your repairs to the test," Han said, firing the repulsors.

The *Millennium Falcon* rose majestically from the ground and pivoted perfectly on its axis before blasting into the air.

Soon they were back where they belonged, in the stars.

"What now?" Meech asked, appearing in the cockpit doorway.

Han checked the controls to make sure they weren't being followed. "Now we drop you at the nearest way station and say our fond farewells."

"And that's it?" she said. "Half the folks back there are light-years from home, with no credits to their names."

Han prepared to make the jump to lightspeed. "Not my problem. I got them off the planet. What more do you want?"

Beside him, Chewie rumbled sadly.

Han snorted. "Well, don't blame me. You were the ones who said we didn't have time to bring them."

Meech realized what they were talking about. "The barrels of rhydonium."

He nodded. "We could've sold the barrels and shared the profits, but hey, I was just thinking like a thief, right?"

And with that Han Solo sent the *Millennium Falcon* shooting into hyperspace.

THE END

**CAN YOU GO BACK AND HELP HAN
MAKE A BETTER DECISION?
WHERE WILL THE ADVENTURE LEAD NEXT TIME?**

HAN GOT LUCKY with his first couple of shots, taking down two of Nodo's goons.

Chewie wasn't so fortunate. He picked up the nearest alien, a scrawny Hoopaloo covered head to toe in ruffled feathers, and threw him at a nearby Devaronian. However, before Han could shout out a warning, a blaster bolt clipped Chewie's shoulder. It wasn't enough to stun the Wookiee, but the force knocked Chewbacca off his feet.

Han turned, ready to take out whoever had fired on his friend, when a stun blast struck him square in his chest. His legs folded beneath him and he went down. He moaned, unable to form words, as rough hands grabbed him and dragged him in front of Nodo.

The reptilian grinned down at Han with a mouth full of sharp teeth. "Who are you, kid, and who do you work for?"

WHO DOES HAN SAY HE WORKS FOR?

HIMSELF—TURN TO PAGE 48.

JABBA THE HUTT—TURN TO PAGE 60.

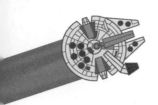

HAN LOOKED AROUND, searching for something that could help. There was a pile of tools nearby, lying next to a junked shuttle. Running over, he found a large hammer. Chewie's eyes went wide as Han tested its durasteel head against his palm and then, with a grunt of exertion, slammed the hammer into the filla-foam.

WHAM!

The hammer just bounced off the hardened shell. Han tried again and again, but it was useless. It was hardly making a dent.

Throwing the hammer aside, Han felt for his own tool belt. There had to be something he could use to free his friend.

WHAT DOES HE USE?

A WELDER—TURN TO PAGE 127.

A SPANNER—TURN TO PAGE 88.

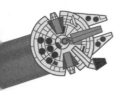

HAN PRESSED THE BUTTON that was supposed to deploy the hidden cannon, and then pressed it again.

It was no good. Chewie hadn't repaired the weapons system yet.

"Give me some good news, buddy!" he yelled into his headset. "Can we take off?"

"HRAAAAH!" Chewie growled over the comm.

"I'll take that as a yes. Buckle up."

Han fired up the engines, and this time they responded. The *Falcon* lurched from the ground. It wasn't the prettiest takeoff, but they were in the air. The ship blasted away from their attackers and soon crossed the threshold into space.

Chewbacca lumbered back into the cockpit, complaining that the power core was likely to blow at any moment.

"We just need it to get us to the next system," Han told him. "There's a way station on Rikmania. We'll pick up a new heat exchanger and be on our way."

In front of him, the comm burbled. Han frowned and answered the call.

"Hello?"

Han's heart sank as a deep gravelly voice rumbled over the speakers.

"Jabba!" he replied, trying to sound cheerful. "How you doing?"

The Hutt got straight to the point, gargling his demands.

"Your cargo?" Han said, thinking of the crates he'd smashed into the TIE fighters. "Of course it's safe. Everything's under control. You know you can trust me, right?"

The sarcastic laugh that echoed from the comm told Han that Jabba didn't trust him at all, and for good reason. Jabba the Hutt was going to make Han and Chewie pay for this. . . .

THE END

**CAN YOU GO BACK AND HELP HAN
MAKE A BETTER DECISION?
WHERE WILL THE ADVENTURE LEAD NEXT TIME?**

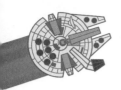

"JABBA THE HUTT?" Nodo threw back his head and laughed heartily. That was not a good sign. "Why would Jabba the Hutt be sneakin' around a shipyard thousands of parsecs from Tatooine?"

It was a good question, and unfortunately Han didn't have a good answer.

"Liar!" Nodo bellowed, snatching a blaster from his belt and aiming it straight at Han.

TURN TO PAGE 90.

IT WASN'T LONG before the repairs on the
Falcon were completed.

Han sighed as he stretched out on the yacht's
overstuffed couch.

He'd miss being Jabba.

Han was used to life as a smuggler, jumping from
job to job, usually on the run from someone. And he
rarely got to enjoy the finer things the galaxy had to
offer.

He felt bad that Chewie was missing out on all the
fancy food and service, but there was no doubt about it:
pretending to be Jabba was great!

There was a polite cough at the door. It was Meech,
holding a platter piled high with bright blue eggs on a
bed of crisp greens.

Han jumped up to take it from her.

"Here, let me help."

"No," she insisted. "It's fine, *Jabba*."

After placing the platter within easy reach of the
couch, Meech turned to leave. She puzzled Han. He'd
seen everyone on the base stripping ships, but not

Meech. She just waited on Nodo and his cronies like a servant.

Han felt an urge to stop her, to ask her about her life, but the eggs she had delivered smelled so good. . . .

WHAT SHOULD HAN DO?

EAT THE FOOD—TURN TO PAGE 94.
TALK TO MEECH—TURN TO PAGE 115.

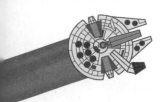

CAVAN SCOTT is one of the writers of *Star Wars*: Adventures in Wild Space and IDW Publishing's *Star Wars* Adventures comic book series. When he's not playing in a galaxy far, far away, Cavan has also written for such popular franchises as Doctor Who, Pacific Rim, Vikings, Star Trek, Adventure Time, and Penguins of Madagascar. You can find him online at www.cavanscott.com.

ELSA CHARRETIER is a French comic book artist and comic book writer. After debuting on C.O.W.L. at Image Comics, Elsa cocreated The Infinite Loop with writer Pierrick Colinet at IDW. She has worked at DC Comics (Starfire, Bombshells, Harley Quinn), launched The Unstoppable Wasp at Marvel, and recently completed the art for the adaptation of *Windhaven* by George R. R. Martin and Lisa Tuttle (Bantam Books). She is currently writing two creator-owned series and has illustrated the first issue of *Star Wars*: Forces of Destiny for IDW.